Katie

W9-DFY-655

SCRAMBLED EGGS Super!

By Dr. Seuss

RANDOM HOUSE · NEW YORK

For LIBBY, ORLO, BRAD and BARRY CHILDS

Copyright 1953 by Dr. Seuss. All rights reserved under International and Pan-American Copyright Conventions. Published in the United States by Random House, Inc., New York, and simultaneously in Canada by Random House of Canada Limited, Toronto.

This title was originally catalogued by the Library of Congress as follows:
Seuss, Dr. Scrambled eggs super. New York, Random House [1953] Tired of scrambled eggs always tasting the same, Peter T. Hooper goes on a great egg hunt for his new recipe. 1. Nonsense verses I. Title. E;Fic 53-5013
ISBN: 0-394-80085-0 (trade hardcover) 0-394-90085-5 (library binding) 0-394-84544-7 (trade paperback)

Manufactured in the United States of America

I don't like to brag and I don't like to boast,
Said Peter T. Hooper, but speaking of toast
And speaking of kitchens and ketchup and cake
And kettles and stoves and the stuff people bake . . .
Well, I don't like to brag, but I'm telling you, Liz,
That speaking of cooks, I'm the best that there is!
Why, only last Tuesday, when mother was out
I really cooked something worth talking about!

You see, I was sitting here, resting my legs
And I happened to pick up a couple of eggs
And I sort of got thinking—it's sort of a shame
That scrambled eggs always taste always the same.

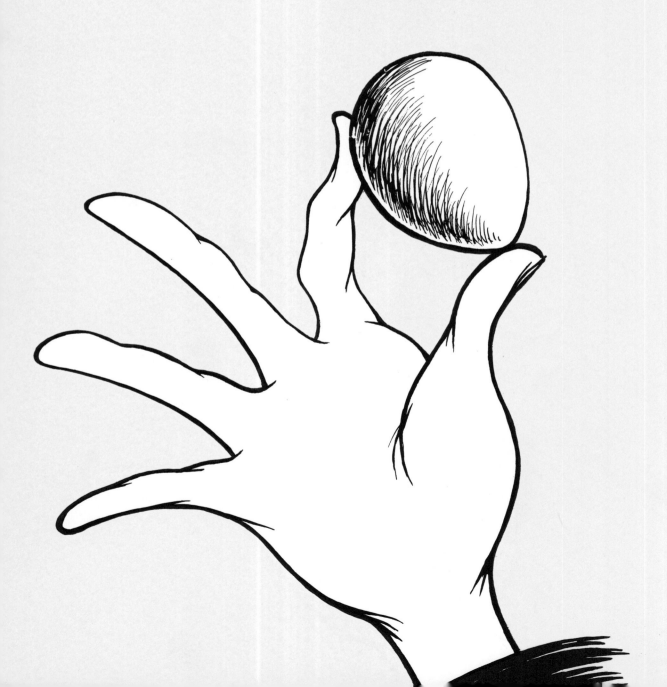

And that's because ever since goodness knows when,
They've always been made from the eggs of a *hen*.
Just a plain common hen! What a dumb thing to use
With all of the *other* fine eggs you could choose!

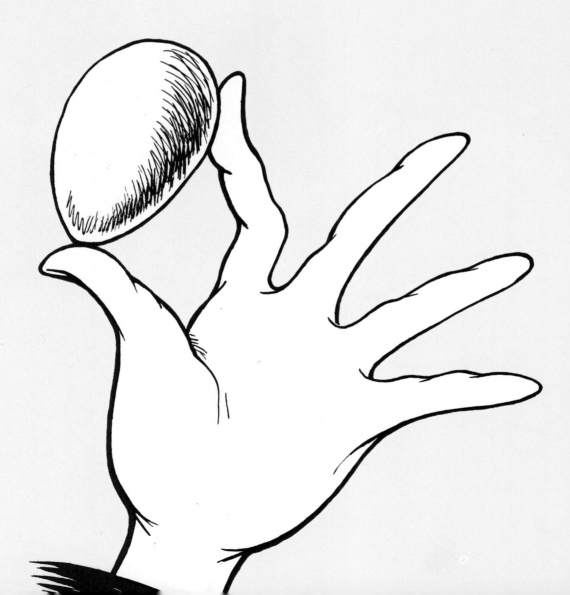

And so I decided that, just for a change,
I'd scramble a *new* kind of egg on the range.
Some fine fancy eggs that no other cook cooks
Like the eggs of the Ruffle-Necked Sala-ma-goox!

A Sala-ma-goox's!
Say! *They* should be good!
So I went out and found some
As quick as I could!

And while I was lugging them back to the house
I happened to notice a Tizzle-Topped Grouse
In a tree down the street. And I knew from her looks
That her egg and the egg of the Sala-ma-goox
Ought to mix mighty well; ought to taste simply super
When scrambled together by Peter T. Hooper.

So I took those eggs home and I frizzled 'em up.
And I added some sugar. Two thirds of a cup.
And a small pinch of pepper. And also a pound
Of horseradish sauce that was sitting around.
And also some nuts.
Then I tasted the stuff
And it tasted quite fine,
But not quite fine enough.

To make the best scramble that's ever been made
A cook has to hook the best eggs ever laid.
So I drove to the country, quite rather far out,
And I studied the birds that were flitting about.
I looked with great care at a Mop-Noodled Finch.
I looked at a Beagle-Beaked-Bald-Headed Grinch.
And, also, I looked at a Shade-Roosting Quail
Who was roosting right under a Lass-a-lack's tail.
And I looked at a Spritz and a Flannel-Wing Jay.
But I just didn't stop. I kept right on my way
'Cause they didn't have eggs. They weren't laying that day.

Then, suddenly . . . *Boy!* Up that hill a short space . . .
Birds! They were laying all over the place!
Great happy gay families with uncles and cousins
All laying fine strictly fresh eggs by the dozens!

Why, I'd have a scramble *more* super than super!
Scrambled eggs Super-dee-Dooper-dee-Booper
Special de luxe à-la-Peter T. Hooper!

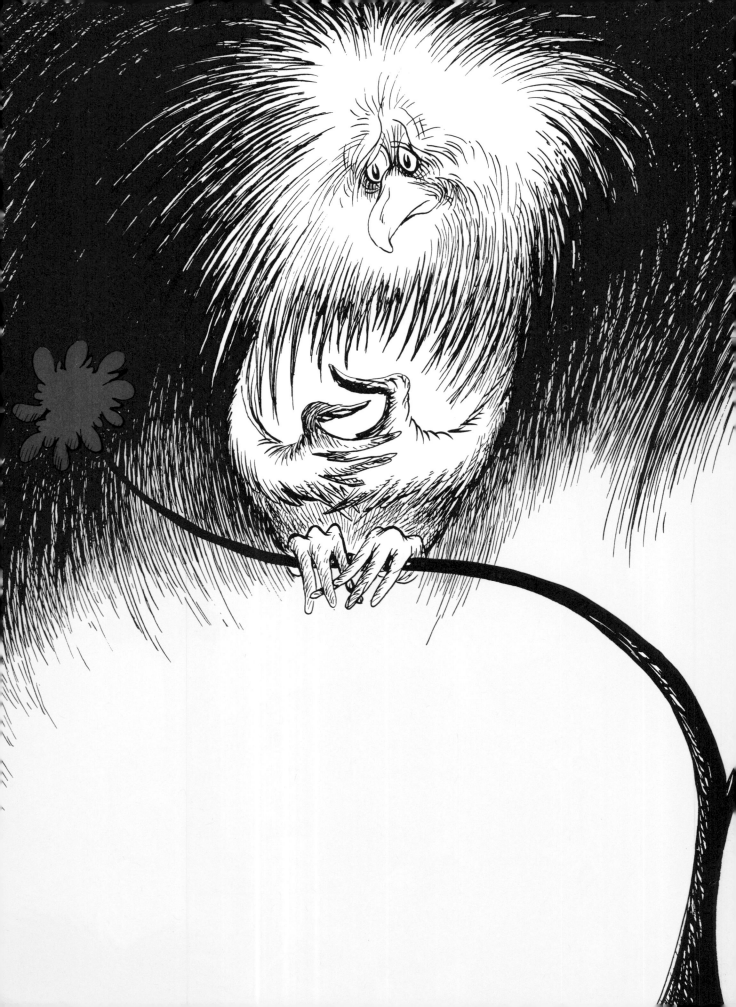

I picked out the eggs in a most careful way.
I only picked those that I knew were Grade-A.
I only took eggs from the very best fowls.
So I didn't take eggs from the Twiddler Owls
'Cause I knew that the eggs of those fellows who twiddle
Taste sort of like dust from inside a bass fiddle.

I went for the kind that were mellow and sweet
And the world's sweetest eggs are the eggs of the Kweet
Which is due to those very sweet trout which they eat
And those trout . . . well, *they're* sweet 'cause they only eat Wogs
And Wogs, after all, are the world's sweetest frogs
And the reason *they're* sweet is, whenever they lunch
It's always the world's sweetest bees that they munch
And the reason no bees can be sweeter than these . . .
They only eat blossoms off Beezlenut Trees
And these Beezlenut Blossoms are sweeter than sweet
And that's why I nabbed several eggs from the Kweet.

But I passed up the eggs of a bird called a Stroodel
Who's sort of a stork, but with fur like a poodle.
For they say that the eggs of this kind of a stork
Are gooey like glue and they stick to your fork,
And the yolks of these eggs, I am told, taste like fleece
While the whites taste like very old bicycle grease.

The places I hiked to! The roads that I rambled
To find the best eggs that have ever been scrambled!
I hunted new birds along wild tangled trails,
Through gullies and gulches, down dingles and dales.
I wriggled my way and I crawled at a creep
Through a forest of ferns that was forty miles deep.
And I mushed through the brush till I found a fine Kwigger
Whose eggs are as big as a pin head, no bigger.

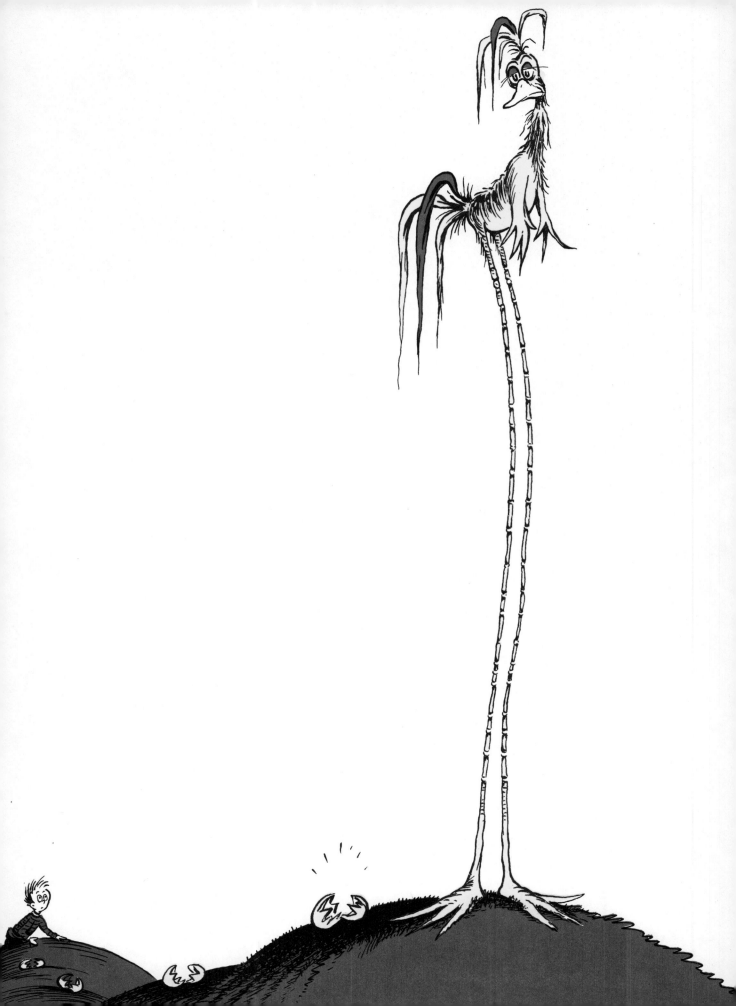

Then I went for the eggs of a Long-Legger Kwong.
Now this Kwong . . . well, she's built just a little bit wrong,
For her legs are so terribly, terribly long
That she has to lay eggs twenty feet in the air
And they drop, with a plop, to the ground from up there!
So unless you can catch 'em before the eggs crash
You haven't got eggs. You've got Long-Legger hash.

Eggs! I'd collected three hundred and two!
But I needed still more! And I suddenly knew
That the job was too big for one fellow to do.
So I telegraphed north to some friends near Fa-Zoal
Which is ten miles or so just beyond the North Pole.
And they all of them jumped in their Katta-ma-Side,
Which is sort of a boat made of sea-leopard's hide,
Which they sailed out to sea to go looking for Grice,
Which is sort of a bird which lays eggs on the ice,
Which they grabbed with a tool which is known as a Squitsch,
'Cause those eggs are too cold to be touched without which.

And while they were sending those eggs, I got word of
A bird that does something that's almost unheard of!
It's hard to believe, but this bird called the Pelf
Lays eggs that are three times as big as herself!
How that Pelf ever learned such a difficult trick
I never found out. But I found that egg quick.
And I managed to get it down out of the nest
And home to the kitchen along with the rest.

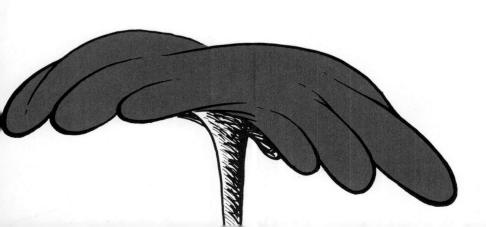

But I didn't stop then, 'cause I knew of some ducks
By the name of the Single-File Zummzian Zuks
Who stroll, single file, through the mountains of Zumms
Quite oddly enough, with their eggs on their thumbs,
And some fellows in Zummz whom I happened to know
Just happened to capture a thousand or so,
And they wrapped up their eggs and they mailed them by air
Marked Special Delivery, Handle with Care.

I needed *more* helpers! And so for assistance
I called up a fellow, named Ali, long distance,
And Ali, as soon as he hung up the phone,
Picked up a small basket and started alone
To climb the steep crags and the jags of Mt. Strookoo
To fetch me the egg of a Mt. Strookoo Cuckoo.
Now these Mt. Strookoo Cuckoos
Are rather small gals . . .

But these Mt. Strookoo Cuckoos have lots of big pals!
They dived from the skies with wild cackling shrieks
And they jabbed at his legs and they stabbed at his cheeks
With their yammering, klammering, hammering beaks,
But Ali, brave Ali, he fought his way through
And he sent me that egg as I knew he would do
For my Scrambled Eggs Super-dee-Dooper-dee-Booper
Special de luxe à-la-Peter T. Hooper!

In the meanwhile, of course, I was keeping real busy
Collecting the eggs of the three-eyelashed Tizzy.
They're quite hard to reach, so I rode on the top
Of a Ham-ikka-Schnim-ikka-Schnam-ikka Schnopp.

Then I found a great flock of South-West-Facing Cranes
And I guess they've got something that's wrong with their brains.
For this kind of a crane, when she's guarding her nest,
Will always stand facing precisely South West.
So to get at those eggs wasn't hard in the least.
I came from behind. From, precisely, North East.

And I captured the egg of a Grickily Gractus
Who lays 'em up high in a prickily cactus.

Then I went for some Ziffs. They're exactly like Zuffs,
But the Ziffs live on cliffs and the Zuffs live on bluffs.
And, seeing how bluffs are exactly like cliffs,
It's mighty hard telling the Zuffs from the Ziffs.
But I *know* that the egg that I got from the bluffs,
If it wasn't a Ziff's from the cliffs, was a Zuff's.

Now I needed the egg of a Moth-Watching Sneth
Who's a bird who's so big she scares people to death!
And this awful big bird . . . Well, the reason they name her
The Moth-Watching Sneth is 'cause that's how they tame her.
She likes watching moths. Sort of quiets her mind.
And while she is watching you sneak up behind
And you yank out her egg. So I got one, of course,
With the help of some friends and a very fast horse.

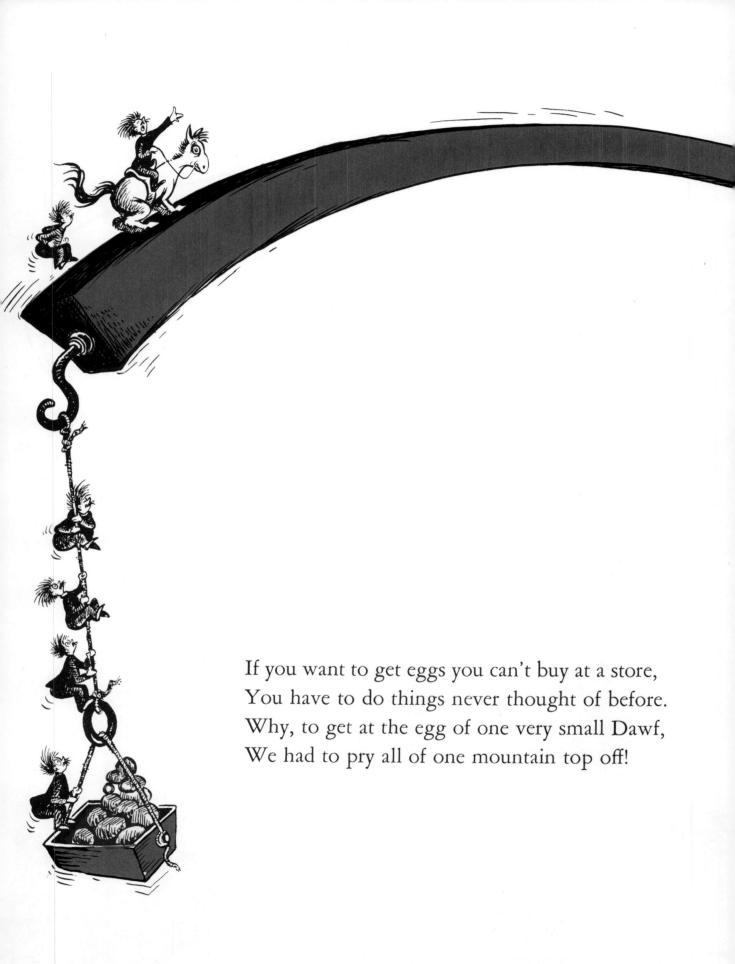

If you want to get eggs you can't buy at a store,
You have to do things never thought of before.
Why, to get at the egg of one very small Dawf,
We had to pry all of one mountain top off!

Then I heard of some birds who lay eggs, if you please,
That taste like the air in the holes in Swiss cheese
And they live in big Zinzibar-Zanzibar trees.
So I ordered a tree full. The job was immense,
But I needed those eggs, and said hang the expense!

I still needed one more! And I saved it for last . . .
The egg of the frightful Bombastic Aghast!
And that bird is so mean and that bird is so fast
That I had to escape on a Jill-ikka-Jast
A fleet-footed beast who can run like a deer
But looks sort of different. You steer him by ear.

All through with the searching! All through with the looking!
I had all I needed! And now for the cooking.
I rushed to the kitchen, the place where I'd stacked 'em.
I rolled up my sleeves. I unpacked 'em and cracked 'em
And shucked 'em and chucked 'em in ninety-nine pans.
Then I mixed in some beans. I used fifty-five cans.
Then I mixed in some ginger, nine prunes and three figs
And parsley. Quite sparsely. Just twenty-two sprigs.
Then I added six cinnamon sticks and a clove
And my scramble was ready to go on the stove!

And you know how they tasted?
They tasted just like . . .
Well, they tasted exactly,
Exactly just like . . . like Scrambled eggs Super-
Dee-Dooper-dee-Booper, Special de luxe
à-la-Peter T. Hooper.

BOOKS BY DR. SEUSS

And to Think That I Saw It on Mulberry Street
The 500 Hats of Bartholomew Cubbins
The King's Stilts
Horton Hatches the Egg
McElligot's Pool
Thidwick The Big-Hearted Moose
Bartholomew and the Oobleck
If I Ran the Zoo
Scrambled Eggs Super
Horton Hears a Who
On Beyond Zebra
If I Ran the Circus
How the Grinch Stole Christmas
Yertle the Turtle and Other Stories
Happy Birthday to You
The Sneetches and Other Stories
Dr. Seuss's Sleep Book
I Had Trouble in Getting to Solla Sollew
The Cat in the Hat Songbook
I Can Lick 30 Tigers Today and Other Stories
The Lorax
Did I Ever Tell You How Lucky You Are?
Hunches in Bunches
The Butter Battle Book

BEGINNER BOOKS

The Cat in the Hat
The Cat in the Hat Comes Back
One Fish Two Fish Red Fish Blue Fish
Green Eggs and Ham
Hop on Pop
Dr. Seuss's ABC
Fox in Socks
The Foot Book
My Book About Me
Mr. Brown Can Moo! Can You?
Marvin K. Mooney, Will You Please Go Now?
The Shape of Me and Other Stuff
There's A Wocket in My Pocket
Great Day for Up
Oh, The Thinks You Can Think
The Cat's Quizzer
I Can Read With My Eyes Shut
Oh Say Can You Say?